Soul Riders

Storybooks for Your Inner Child

DocDocFoose

Soul Riders

Storybooks for Your Inner Child

DocDocFoose

This is a work of fiction. Names, characters, places, and incidents are products of the author's imagination or are used fictitiously. Any resemblance to actual persons, living or dead, or actual events is purely coincidental.

PALMETTO
PUBLISHING
Charleston, SC
www.PalmettoPublishing.com

Copyright© 2024 by Ladan Foose

Illustrated using Midjourney Pro

All rights reserved.

This book or any portion thereof may not be reproduced or used in any manner whatsoever without the express written permission of the publisher except for the use of brief quotations in a book review.

Hardcover ISBN: 9798822962910
Paperback ISBN: 9798822962927
eBook ISBN: 9798822962934

Dedication

"The wound is the place where the Light enters you."
— Rumi

To all our inner children —
May you be healed as you exit the shadows.

Introduction

Please read before you begin.

Welcome to Soul Riders, a series of stories for the inner child that addresses complex issues holding adults back from realizing our limitless human potential. While the characters are fictitious, the stories reflect real experiences and emotions. Each narrative is informed by the unique energy of its respective locale, as experienced by the author during travels. You'll walk alongside captivating characters, each embarking on their own healing journey, while a mysterious master storyline unfolds across the series.

These stories are intended for an adult audience and explore the impact of trauma on humanity. While these narratives aim to offer insight and understanding, they may evoke or unearth strong emotions or memories. If at any point you find yourself feeling overwhelmed or activated, please pause and care for yourself in the ways that feel most supportive to you. The support of a mental health professional can be helpful in processing any feelings that arise. Your well-being is most important, so please engage with these stories intentionally, perhaps in a quiet space of your own.

Wishing you the highest good throughout your journey, wherever it may lead you.

Contents

			Discussion Questions
Soul Riders Vol 1	1-41		115
Soul Riders Vol 2	43-74		116
Soul Riders Vol 3	77-112		117

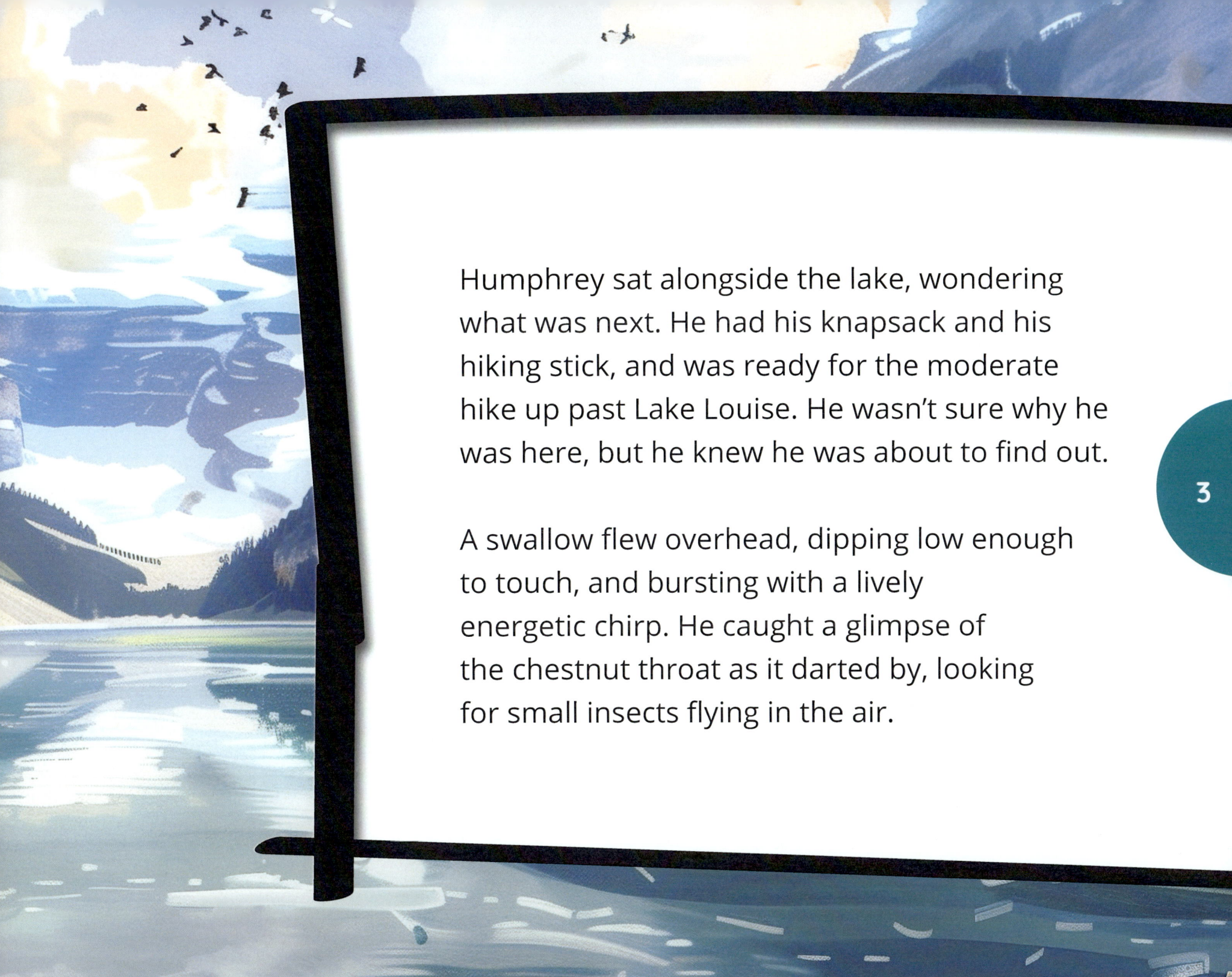

Humphrey sat alongside the lake, wondering what was next. He had his knapsack and his hiking stick, and was ready for the moderate hike up past Lake Louise. He wasn't sure why he was here, but he knew he was about to find out.

A swallow flew overhead, dipping low enough to touch, and bursting with a lively energetic chirp. He caught a glimpse of the chestnut throat as it darted by, looking for small insects flying in the air.

Humphrey looked up at the cliff face, covered in trees at the top, rocky slopes bending down to kiss the lake's edge. He saw the way the ice, still trapped at the bottom edges, formed small triangles, their points narrowing in and tracing the skirt of the mountain where it touched the water. On a day like today where the sky was clear and still and the sun bright, the lake was a mirror to the mountain itself. And so these triangular bits of ice flowed into a mirror of their likeness, forming arrowheads all along the edge of the lake. These arrowheads pointed, Humphrey knew, to where he was supposed to go next. He started walking.

That's when he felt it again. The gentle tug. Humphrey had come to recognize its tingly sensation, sparked in his core and then running like electricity along his skin, raising the hairs and goosebumps with a current so alive he no longer wanted to resist it. But it hadn't started that way.

5

Stanley unwrapped the package and set it on the living room table. It was a hunting knife he had bought his husband, spending at least two hours in the store, looking across the different options and admiring the form of the blades and the handles, some with sleek modern looks and some with carvings. His attention had finally landed on a beautiful Maplewood carved knife handle, its blade simple but edged to a sharp brilliance. He was excited to see the look on Humphrey's face when he arrived home for their anniversary.

He would wrap it closer to 7 o'clock, when he expected Humphrey home from his investment banking role, exhausted and yet never done for the day. Stanley hummed to himself as he walked up their three-story Manhattan apartment and into the heated steam shower— the last time he would walk those floors.

It wasn't until years later that Humphrey realized it was his own knife. The trauma of that night, coming home at 9 o'clock to the police and neighbors swarming outside his apartment, had blocked out any reasoning through the details. He had been late (again), letting meeting after meeting and a few emergency phonecalls fill his evening before he realized he was going to be late for his own anniversary. He grabbed his heavy wool overcoat and the bottle of champagne his admin had purchased and headed briskly out the door.

The trauma of discovering what awaited him had masked any thought of that strange, ornate knife and why someone breaking into a New York City upper east side apartment would have that kind of expensive, tasteful hunting knife on them. A knife he would have loved if it hadn't been coated in red.

Even as his mind exploded into a frenzy of disbelief, denial and anger that night, something else stopped him short— a deep, quiet calm inside that he felt for the first time in the hospital critical care waiting room. And that was how it all started for him.

Humphrey picked up his knapsack and slung it over his back, bracing his injured foot against a large rock as he rewrapped the bandages around the sprain. The sprain had happened as he reached for the blue egg inside the high-set nest the prior day. He had been proud of himself for climbing up that high—something he hadn't done since his early boyhood days at this grandparents' ranch in Wisconsin. Unfortunately, taking his attention from the tree and the nest led to a slip, and his ankle landed hard and awkwardly when he regained his footing. But he had the egg, and added it gently to the other oddities he had been asked to collect into his knapsack.

He listened carefully for the next message, looking across the expanse of Lake Louise to the crested ridges, dipping down into a valley of exquisite beauty.

The reflection of the mountains in the water reminded him of his own reflection as a young adolescent, looking into the swimming pool while other boys jeered at him, having stolen his swim trunks and bullying him to jump into the freezing pool. Hiding his own shame would have almost driven him to do it, but the anger inside him warmed him up and instead he turned back to them, open and wild in his naked state, roaring both out loud and physically with every fiber of his being at the injustice of it all.

He ran then, like he had never run before. Instead of running to his locker to get a change of clothes, he just ran and ran until he became a streak of color that no one could see. Finally invisible. Finally able to redefine himself. Running until he was finally the upstanding Harvard MBA and top triathlete his family, college friends, and empty relationships all expected him to be.

Humphrey was 29 before he ever truly fell in love. Handsome in a plain, boyish way, with a shaved head and beautiful warm smile, Stanley was not who he expected to meet when he walked into the coffee shop in London. Six whirlwind months later and he couldn't imagine his life without him. Their love is what made him strong enough to finally come out to his family and friends, some of whom he never saw again, as the muscular triathlete image they had of him did not coalesce with him being homosexual.

Humphrey took a deep breath and relaxed his mind, feeling into his body as he had learned to do. Running his thoughts gently over his muscles, skin, nerves, sensing and relaxing any tensions. Then he could feel It. The air thickened in that familiar way and there It was. It looked at him, smiled gently, and asked him how he was doing. Felzer, as he had come to call It, was small and green most of the time, appearing to him almost like he imagined a leprechaun would be, and glowing. Always glowing. But apparently not always green or small.

He had enough conversations with Felzer by now to know that It wasn't locked into one form, and just adopted something simple and appropriate for the occasion. It had taken a long time after the shock of their first contact for Humphrey to learn the technique that would bring him into Felzer's presence. Or rather, to realize Felzer's presence and be able to actually see and communicate with It. Because one of the earliest things he had learned was that Felzer was a Soul Rider. Always there, almost always invisible.

17

When the doctors announced the flatline, Humphrey just stood up and walked out. Walked straight out of the ICU, straight past his car, straight out of the hospital lot. Straight out of his mind. He started to run, his powerful, massive muscles responding instantly after a lifetime of training. The faster he ran the less he had to think. Not about the traffic, the honking swerving cars, the people yelling. He ran until he collapsed, he knew not where. He didn't care.

He opened his eyes in the morning to find he had collapsed in an abandoned field he didn't recognize. *Good, at least no one will find me.* His body lay there on the cold ground, waiting for death, because there was no reason to do anything anymore, including eating or drinking. He wished he could stop breathing but he knew it would only take a few days anyway. And he could wait; he had built up that learned endurance earlier in life by necessity.

As he lay there, accepting and relaxing into what he knew would be his end, he realized his body had never been this relaxed. Surprising, given how cold the ground was. Normally someone would stiffen and curl up, muscles tightening to constrict blood vessels and folding in on oneself to reduce loss of warmth.

So this is what it feels like to relax into death. Strange.

22

That's when he felt It. Something else was there with him. Enveloping him. No, inside him... He wasn't sure. There was an outside-inside feel to It.

✧ *I'm here.*

Humphrey became very still. His body was already very relaxed but now he was still, including his mind which became very quiet. Had he imagined it? What was that?

✧ *Ha ha! No, not imagining.*

Oh my god, this is how I lose it.

✧ *Not losing it. I am Felzer.*

What?! Well, if I'm going to lose my shit, I'm going to do it sitting up.

Humphrey raised himself up onto his arms and instantly vomited. He sat there, listening, straining to hear that voice again. The voice that wasn't a voice because it wasn't a sound outside of himself, but he didn't know what else to call it. Slowly, he realized he wasn't going to hear it again. But he noticed as he sat in his own vomit that he didn't really want to die this way. There had to be some pills to OD on back at home. So he stood up, and marched to his own death, strangely warm given the night he had spent in the field.

I need you to do something. That's how Felzer started the conversation with him a month ago. And then through a complicated series of mind images and sounds, Felzer explained.

Humphrey had learned over the years that Felzer struggled with language, or maybe just didn't like to talk, who knows. So it was a mix of words, gestures, images, sounds, even feelings that It communicated with, all from inside Humphrey so no one else could see it. Apparently that was part of being a Soul Rider. Always there, always listening, Felzer was part of Humphrey and had been from the moment he was born. A portal had opened, allowing Felzer access to choose Humphrey. Given Its lack of interest in talking, there wasn't much more that Humphrey knew.

25

He had asked Felzer all the questions he could think of...
Why me? Who / What are you? Why do you look that way? Why can't anyone else see you? Why did you come to me that day?

I did not come. I was there. Always there. Felzer pointed Its finger and moved Its arm to show what Humphrey had come to realize was an odd S-like symbol. *I was there in the gap. I am yours. You are mine. That is why. Soul Rider.*

What the fuck is a Soul Rider?! Does everyone have one? Felzer looked at Humphrey with an odd mischievous-loving look, placing Its hand to the right of Its nose and pointing one finger up into the air and smiling as though Humphrey had asked the question as a joke and expected no answer.

Humphrey realized that when he asked questions, he could get a range of responses: clear, cryptic, no response, or that infuriating mischievous-loving finger-pointing smile. And when Humphrey got really irritated and worked up, Felzer would just disappear. He thought that was just like a petulant, magical, soul-riding leprechaun, or whatever the hell It was, disappearing whenever there's an argument. But he learned over time that Felzer wasn't the one disappearing; it was Humphrey himself whose irritation would disturb his mind so much he could no longer sense Felzer. Over time, as he learned to become quiet in his body and mind, he was able to always access and see Felzer. Though that didn't mean his questions were always answered.

29

30

Felzer, I have everything, though that egg was a mother fucker to get. Phew! Alright, look.

Felzer leaned down with a smile to look in the knapsack. Humphrey realized yet again that Felzer was humoring him by "looking" given that Felzer knew everything Humphrey did, said, thought as soon as he did (and sometimes it felt like before). It only took a physical form so Humphrey would have a more familiar way to connect and a place to "land" his mind when he was communicating.

Humphrey found himself wishing his ankle was healed and then felt that familiar warm energy wrapping around his ankle. He realized then he hadn't really wished it; it's more that he knew it would happen. It often did with Felzer. That healing energy was just another surprise part of the journey he had learned over the past years. It was one of the things that had helped him relax into trusting that this weird thing inside-outside him wasn't some evil invasion.

Lean into the crazy. That had been Humphrey and his team's go-to phrase when rowing in college, pushing their arms and bodies beyond the limit even as their lungs screamed for oxygen. *Lean into the crazy.* He had adopted it again when thinking about Felzer's "appearance" in his life. He had come to trust this weird little leprechaun that had saved his life again and again.

33

34

Felzer began rubbing Its hands together as if to warm them. Humphrey mirrored the motion in a silent act they had perfected over the years. As Felzer separated Its hands from one another, a warm glow started to form in the space between them. At the same time, the space between Humphrey's hands began to change. Softly at first, as if looking through a mist, and then the image began to sharpen as Humphrey let go more in his mind and relaxed into it. Bigger and bigger it expanded until it was the size of an opening that could narrowly fit Humphrey's large frame.

That's when he saw it. Humphrey paused to squint. His focus faltering, the image began to dissipate. *Let go. Not hold.* Felzer gently guided Humphrey, who relaxed again. And what he saw amazed him. Something so expansive and yet constantly in motion. *An ocean of waterfalls?* his mind whispered. No. That makes no sense. *A large blue sphere with no limits?* No. He shook his head, trying to clear his mind again. He couldn't make sense of what he was seeing.

37

Then he closed his eyes and looked again with Felzer's help. The fog lifted and he saw the beautiful garden clearly. Trees and blossoms as far as the eye could see, with a beautiful feast table laid out in the middle.

And there, standing and smiling, was Stanley. *It's here. It's really here.* A final shred of despair escaped from Humphrey in the sound of a sob, and every fiber of his being filled with and sang in joy.

Door is ready. Felzer smiled at him deeply. And disappeared forever for Humphrey.

39

40

41

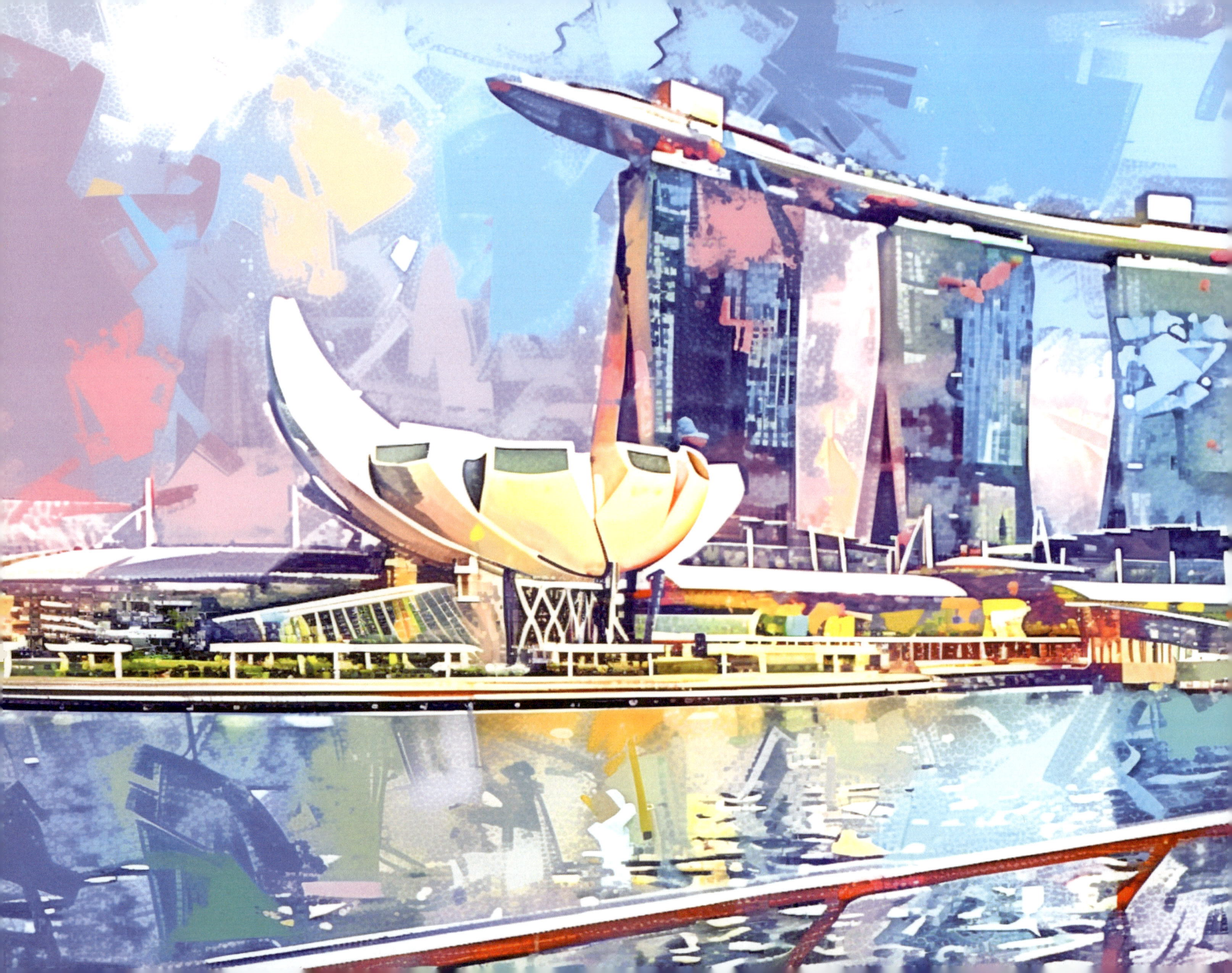

Soul Riders

Volume 2

44

Bai Fei stopped by the water's edge, looking at the boats along the Marina Bay. She had never seen a more beautiful sight, with the water illuminated by the light show and the moon shining as a crescent in the sky.

She hoped the next day would be as glorious as what she had experienced today. It was the first time she had crested. A soul crest had been her one thought for the past four years of training, but only when she let go did she finally become what she had always been seeking.

Bai Fei smiled and began wheeling to the high-rise apartment where she lived with her cat.

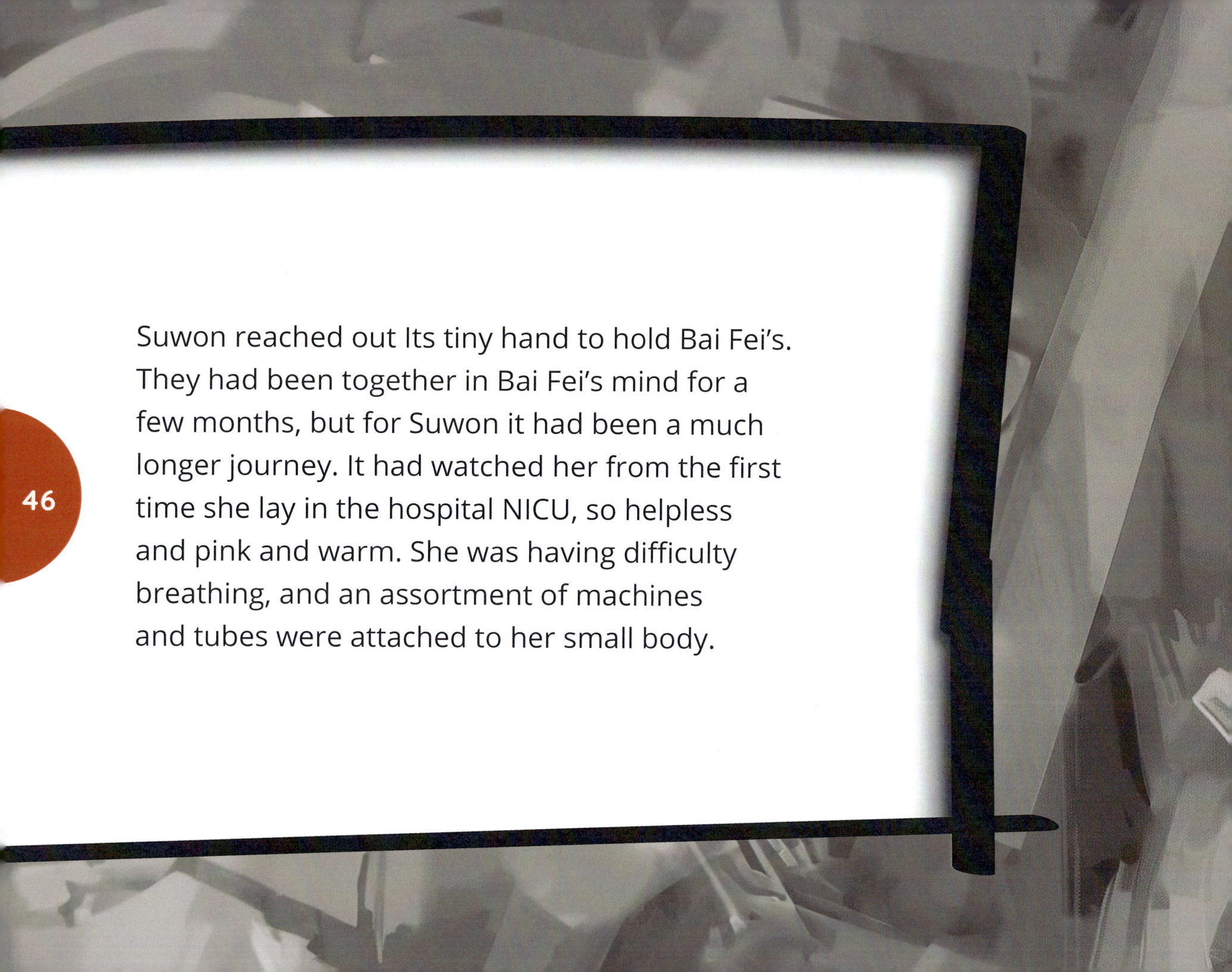

Suwon reached out Its tiny hand to hold Bai Fei's. They had been together in Bai Fei's mind for a few months, but for Suwon it had been a much longer journey. It had watched her from the first time she lay in the hospital NICU, so helpless and pink and warm. She was having difficulty breathing, and an assortment of machines and tubes were attached to her small body.

47

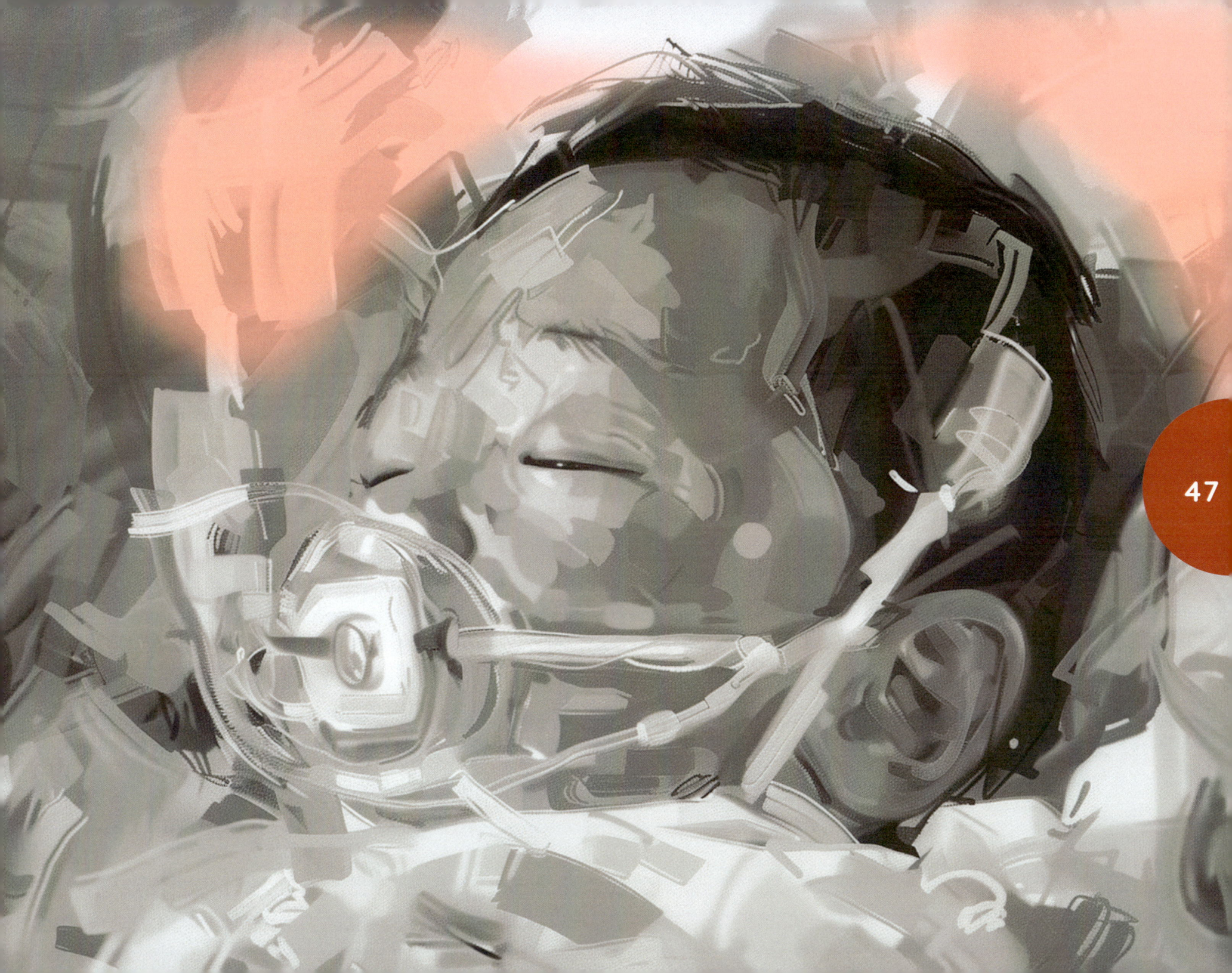

48

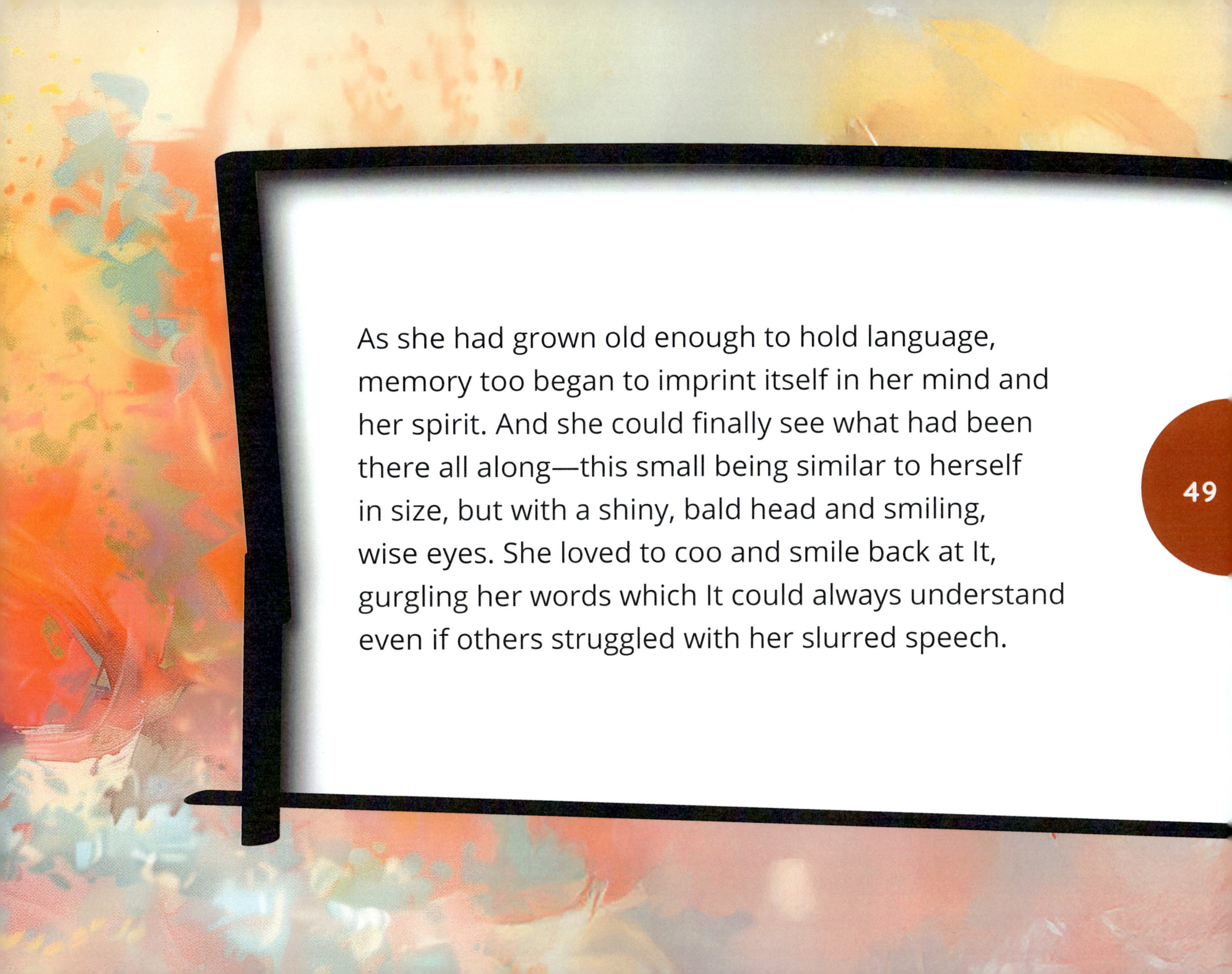

As she had grown old enough to hold language, memory too began to imprint itself in her mind and her spirit. And she could finally see what had been there all along—this small being similar to herself in size, but with a shiny, bald head and smiling, wise eyes. She loved to coo and smile back at It, gurgling her words which It could always understand even if others struggled with her slurred speech.

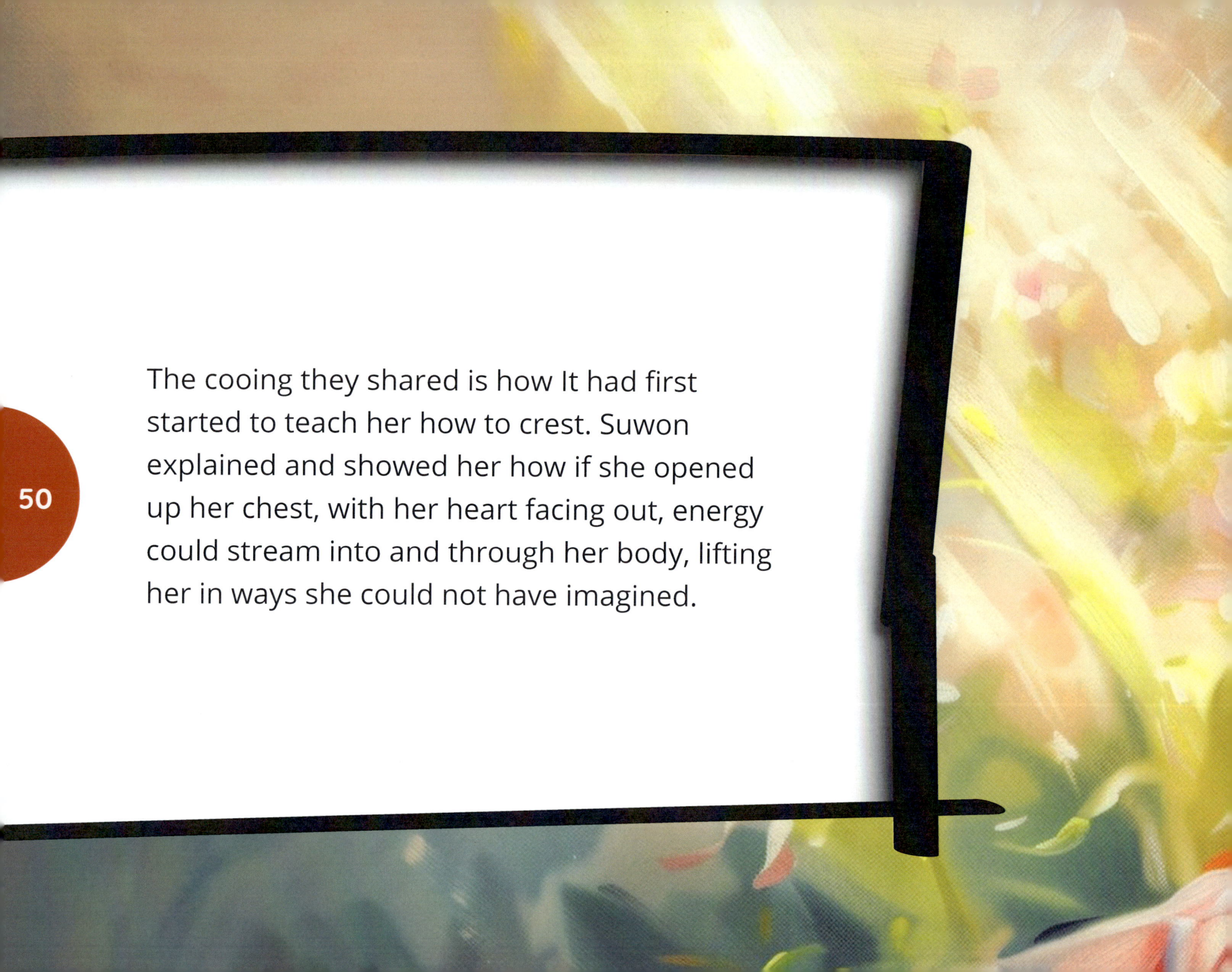

The cooing they shared is how It had first started to teach her how to crest. Suwon explained and showed her how if she opened up her chest, with her heart facing out, energy could stream into and through her body, lifting her in ways she could not have imagined.

51

52

Even if her small body was confined to a wheelchair, the first time she felt the soul crest she couldn't stop smiling because it felt like her whole body was alight with a glowing, throbbing energy. She didn't feel constrained or trapped; she felt a type of freedom few ever experience even if they can freely walk, run, or fly. But she only felt it when Suwon did it for her, and she wanted so badly to master it herself.

Bai Fei didn't know it but she had been seeking Suwon in every moment. In every step, every miss after a hard effort, every bead of frustration on her small forehead, she had been searching for It. The one who would help explain why things were as they were, and how she could best deal with them. The one she could always turn to when things felt so hard that she just wanted it to all go away and end. The one who eased all her "standard" human frustrations, and helped her breathe clearly and openly again, so that the world didn't feel like it was weighing down and crushing her chest.

55

56

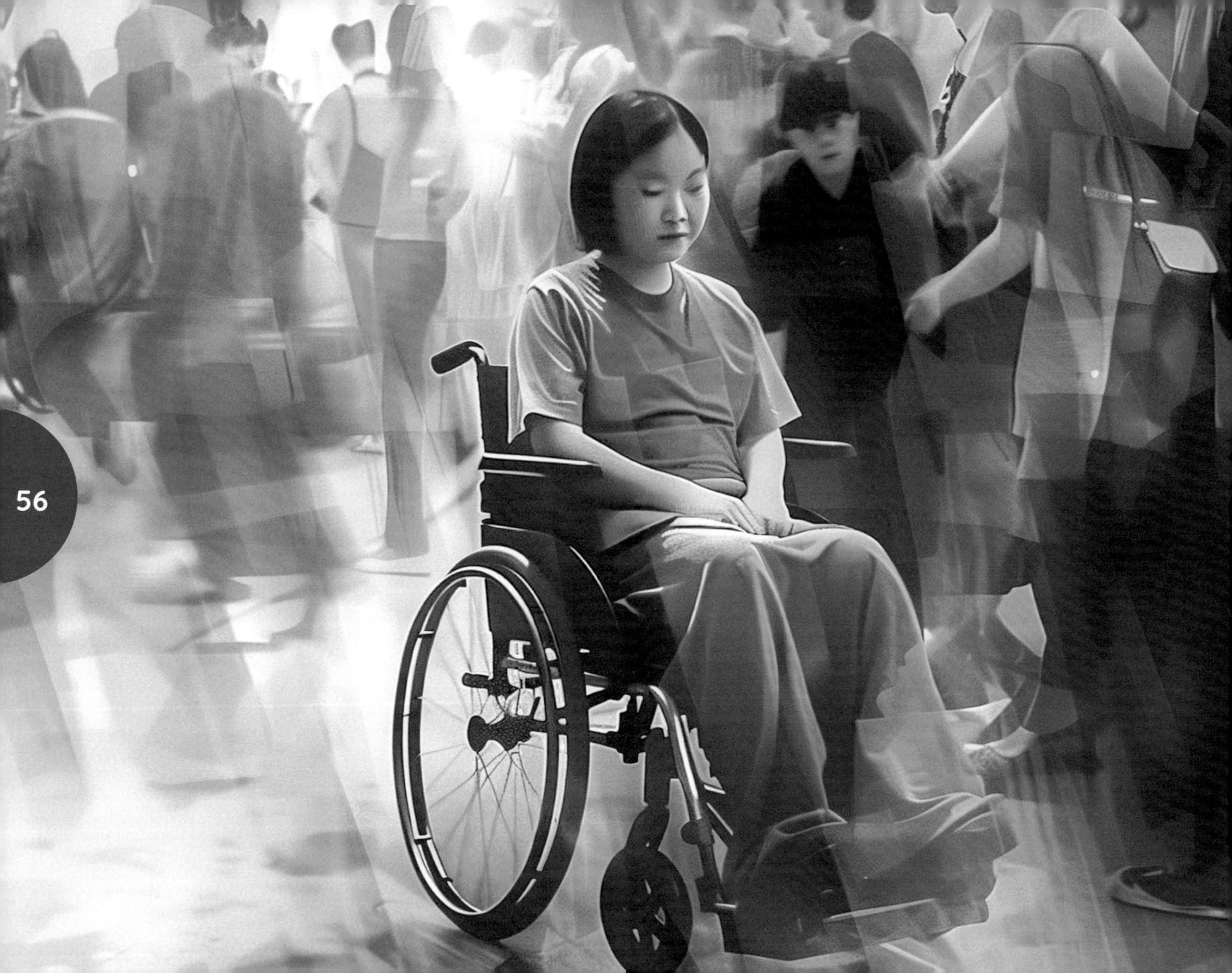

As she grew older, Bai Fei began to realize that others didn't see her as clearly as Suwon did. Whether overlooked and ignored, treated awkwardly, or directly harassed and put down, so many people saw her as "other". Without the benefits of "standard" human mobility, she stood out in a crowd, in a room, in a relationship.

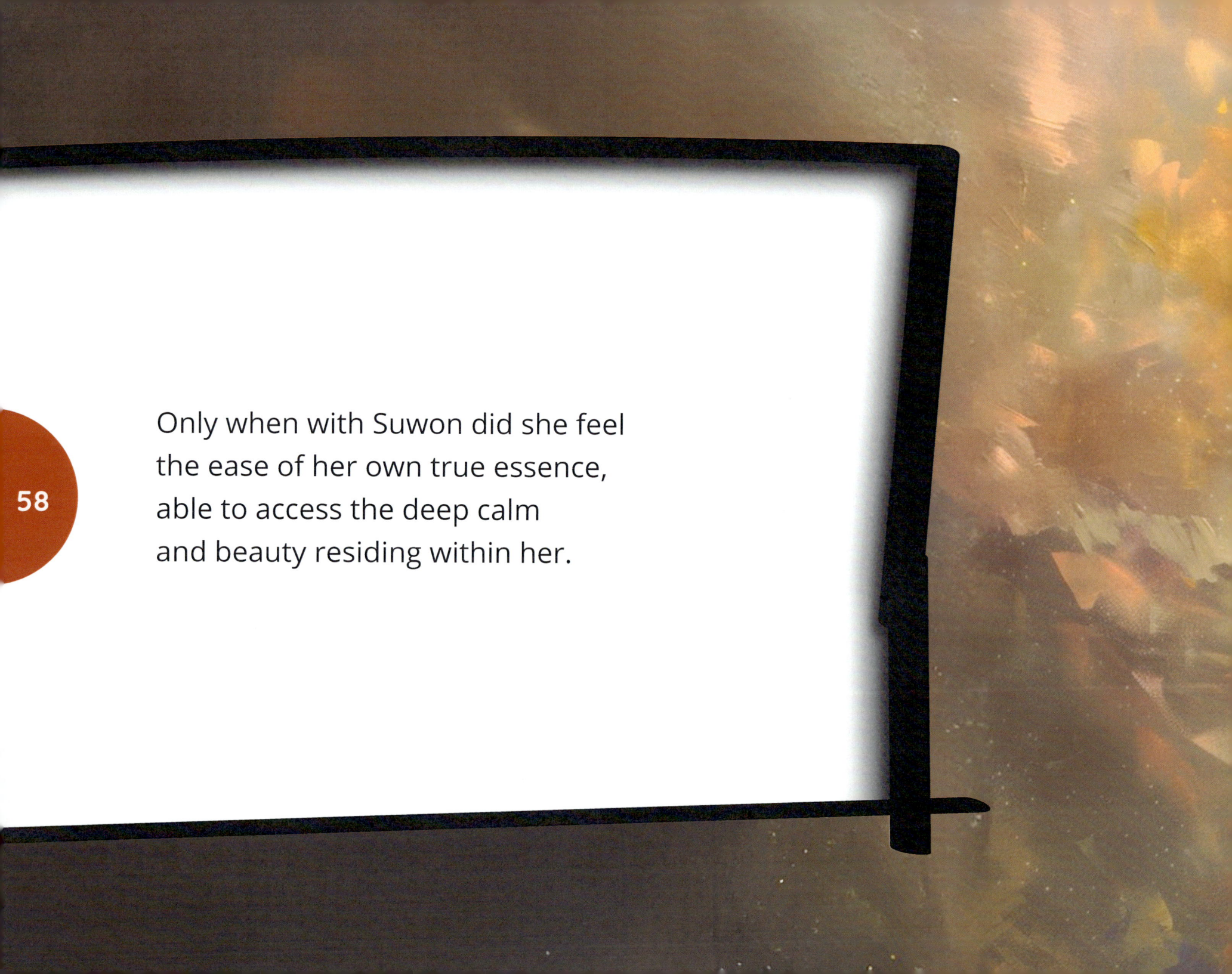

Only when with Suwon did she feel
the ease of her own true essence,
able to access the deep calm
and beauty residing within her.

59

60

It was when she was crying one day after a bad incident on the bus that Suwon showed her the first step.

With a series of hand and arm motions, combined with a rhythmic intake and exhale of Its breath, It showed her the first elevation step of the soul crest. She realized as It kept repeating the motion that It was expecting her to follow, so she started slowly and carefully trying to mimic each gesture. Her motor control made it difficult, and after two hours of non-stop trying she was too tired to keep going.

But as she let go into the process and tried again with Suwon the next day, and the next, and the next… she began to master every small movement with the precision of poetry. What looked like a graceful arc of the arm was actually masterful and consistent motor control to a degree that would not even have been detectable to the human eye, nor been possible for most "standard" human bodies.

63

64

After the first elevation, came the rising, the resting, the arcing, the crescent, and many other sub-moves to make up the eleven total master movements required for the soul crest. Following four years of careful study under the tutelage of Suwon, Bai Fei was ready to do it on her own. That day near the Marina Bay was the first time she had accomplished it. After a 2-minute crest that felt like an eternity, she came down the other side, energized, elated, and full of so much clear-running joy and power that she was beside herself. Suwon looked at her curiously and smiled. It signaled her to rest and that she would have another opportunity the next day.

That night Bai Fei tossed and turned in her sleep, having a vision of being trapped in a dark box and not knowing which way was out. She was terrified and exhausted in the dream, utterly alone.

67

68

That's when she heard the gentle cooing that had been her shared language with Suwon since she was first verbal. The cooing was persistent and getting louder. And as she listened to it, the darkness began to ebb away and she could see a faint outline becoming more and more bright — a way forward in the dark.

Following her instincts, Bai Fei began in the dream world to go through the motions of the soul crest. And as she edged towards the eleventh movement, she felt the earth around her give way, as a boundless joy lifted her from her dream and back into the waking world where she was floating. Looking down at her bed and her surprised cat, she could see the warm glowing edges of a portal.

71

72

73

She walked down the hallway, passing door after door. Light filled every part of the infinite corridor, reflecting off all the doors which were sealed. But as She walked up to the most recent door, She noticed a small crack, letting the light seep out to what lay beyond. And She smiled.

75

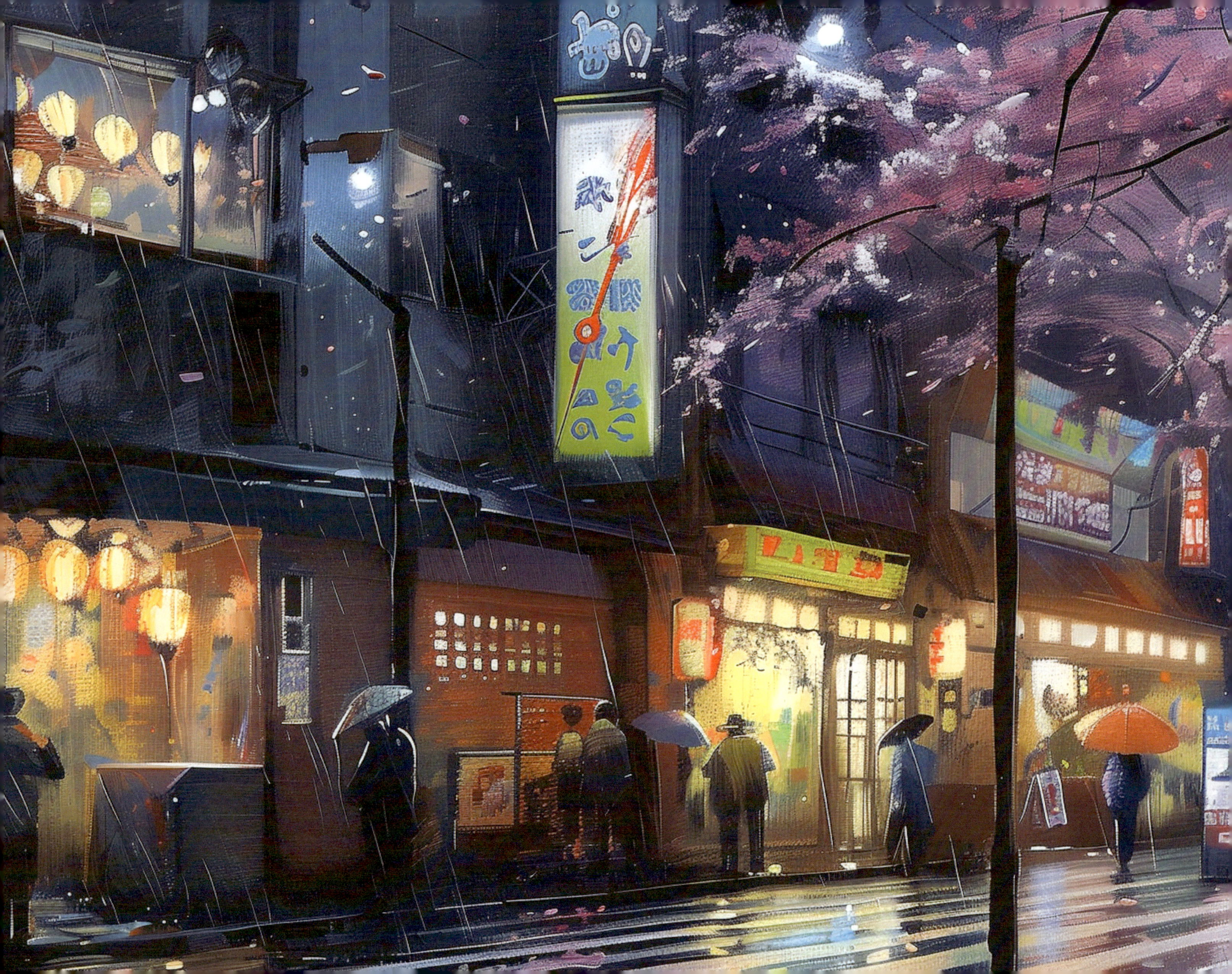

Soul Riders

Volume 3

78

"Meet Holly," Yuka said in an even tone. "She's the new me."

Glancing in the mirror, she twirled as she enjoyed the electric blue felt of her skirt, the flowing pink extensions in her pigtails. She felt beautiful, finally.

Wink. She could almost hear the bright ding of an anime bell in her head. Her life was finally coming together, everything in its place, including her new job, just like in her favorite manga comic.

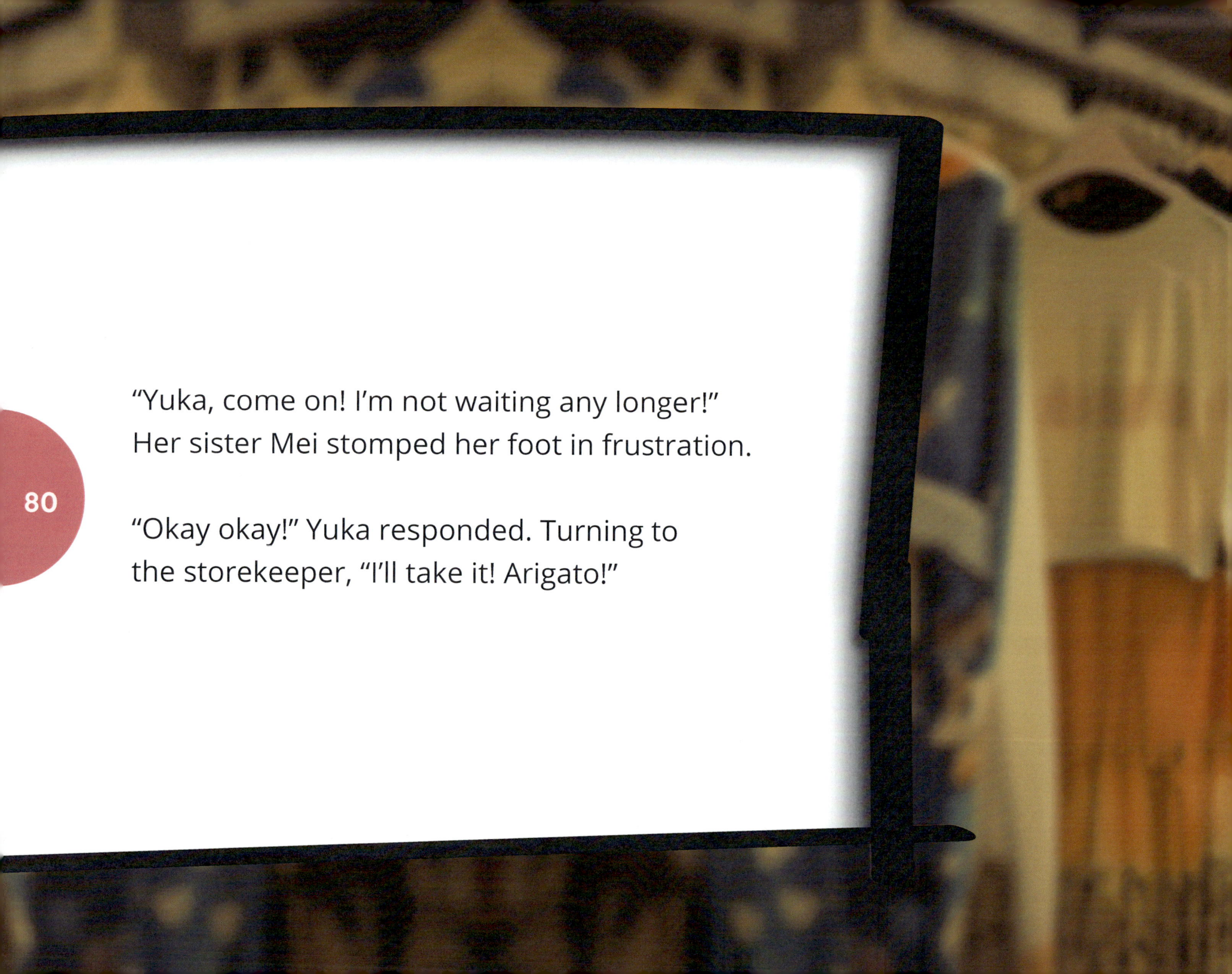

"Yuka, come on! I'm not waiting any longer!" Her sister Mei stomped her foot in frustration.

"Okay okay!" Yuka responded. Turning to the storekeeper, "I'll take it! Arigato!"

81

82

Yuka's elation lasted about as long as it usually did; that is to say, it ended on Monday when she returned to work. Gregory, her gaijin boss, gave her his usual creepy smile as he sidled up next to her in the office.

"Hey, beautiful," he crooned, his whisper wet and heavy against her ear.

"Hello, Gregory-san! I hope you had a nice weekend," she smiled as she stiffened in anticipation of what he might have in store for her today.

"I love that pink in your hair. So sexy." He fingered her hair as he massaged her shoulder.

When someone walked into the shared office space, he quickly took a step away from her.

But she knew he would be back. He always came back. They always came back.

85

86

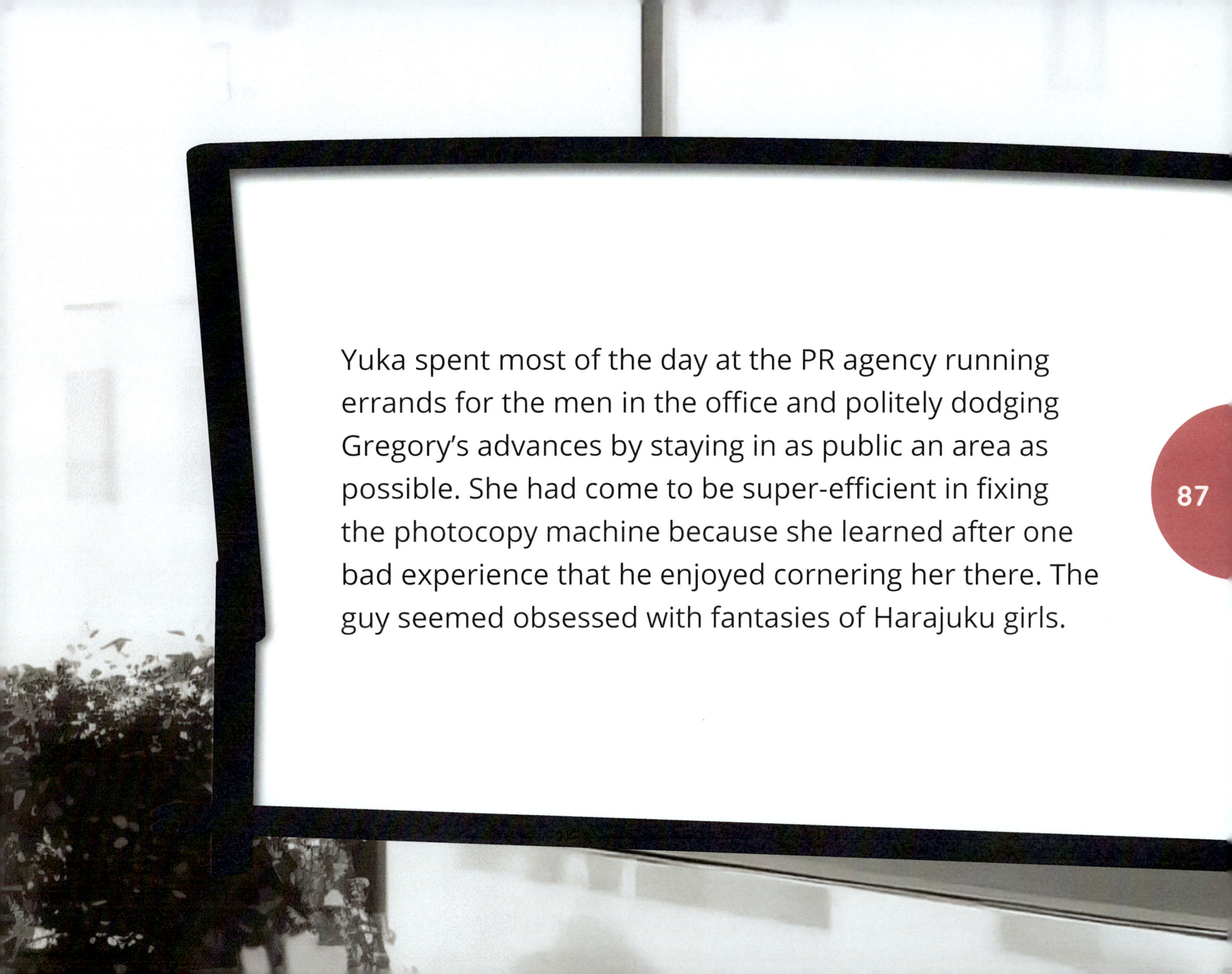

Yuka spent most of the day at the PR agency running errands for the men in the office and politely dodging Gregory's advances by staying in as public an area as possible. She had come to be super-efficient in fixing the photocopy machine because she learned after one bad experience that he enjoyed cornering her there. The guy seemed obsessed with fantasies of Harajuku girls.

At nights Yuka was in school, taking classes to finally become a writer as she had always wanted. Ever since she was a child living at her uncle's home, she had always dreamt of running away, and stories are what had helped her escape. Stories had the power to lift you out of any hell and into a new world. When Oji would touch her, she would imagine she was somewhere else— a young American girl from Kansas exploring the big open country. Sometimes she'd give her character a name, Holly, and imagine what it would be like to explore all the bright lights and diverse sights, tastes, smells of New York City as Holly.

89

90

Yuka slipped out from work that afternoon to make a run to the grocery store. She also was having a hard time staying in that office. Somehow knowing her new release was coming, a new job, made it harder to put up with all the crap. Like her soul could feel freedom around the corner, away from gropes and "accidental" brush ups against hard-ons in the photocopy room. That particular day had been especially difficult. With much of the office working on a new campaign in a collaborative workroom, there hadn't been many other people to run interference between her and Gregory. He had been even more aggressive than usual.

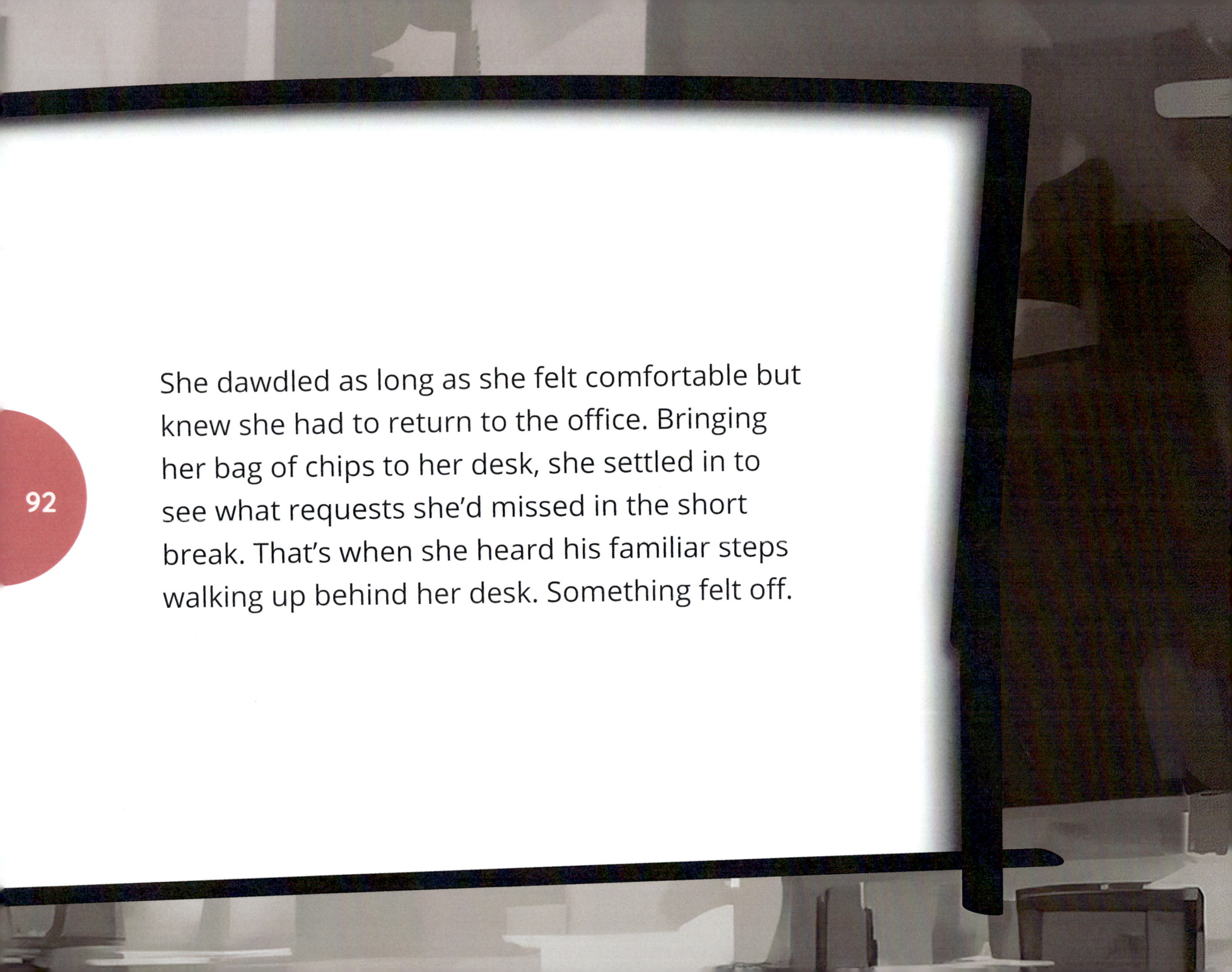

She dawdled as long as she felt comfortable but knew she had to return to the office. Bringing her bag of chips to her desk, she settled in to see what requests she'd missed in the short break. That's when she heard his familiar steps walking up behind her desk. Something felt off.

93

94

Why is it so quiet elsewhere in the office? was the last thought she remembered having. But from the bruise marks on her neck and thighs, it was clear a lot more had happened. She must have blacked out or blocked out. She sat crying in the office bathroom, confused, dazed, and in every kind of pain imaginable.

She remembered all the times she escaped as Holly at Oji's house and tried to picture herself melting away, being replaced by a strong, ordinary American girl. She couldn't do it this time. It was too real— the pain, the stickiness she felt, the sound of his steps and breathing echoing in her skull. Yuka cried out as her innards heaved and everything she had eaten that day came up on the bathroom floor.

Yuka never made it to day one of her new job. Something in her had broken. She stayed in her apartment day in and day out, curtains pulled closed, living off whatever quick foods she had stocked up on from the convenience store.

97

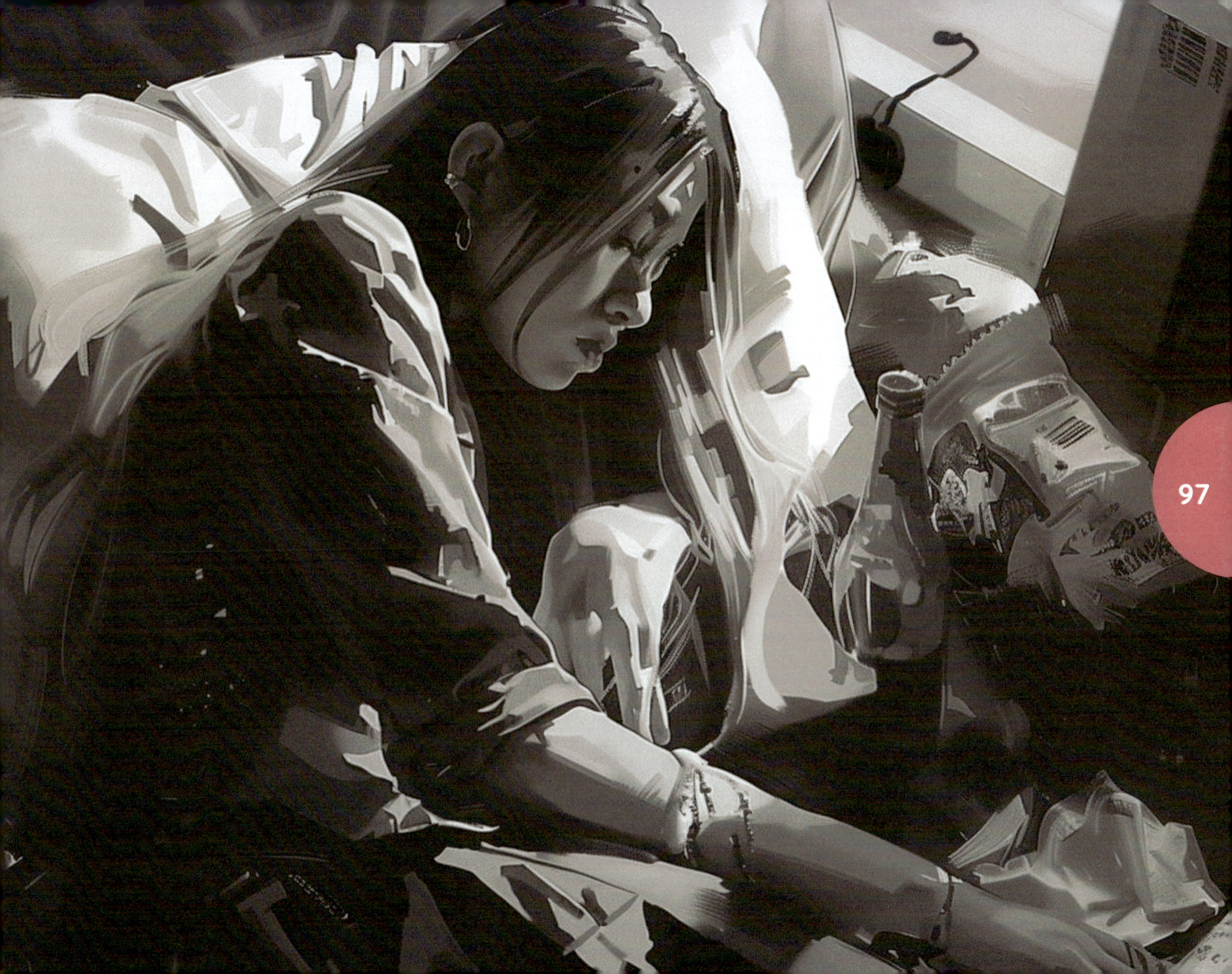

98

Somehow, quietly, things started to change for her three days later. She felt a quiet voice deep inside that wanted to tear free and break into the open.

Was it Holly? No. It felt much more powerful, much more calm—not the fun, high-pitched enthusiasm of youth. And it was less a voice than a feeling, but that she understood as well as if it had been a language.

She asked it what it wanted. But it wanted nothing from her. Yet it was this voice that eventually got her dressed in the morning and out the door, looking more like herself than she'd ever been. She walked to Mei's apartment fifteen minutes away and knocked on the door.

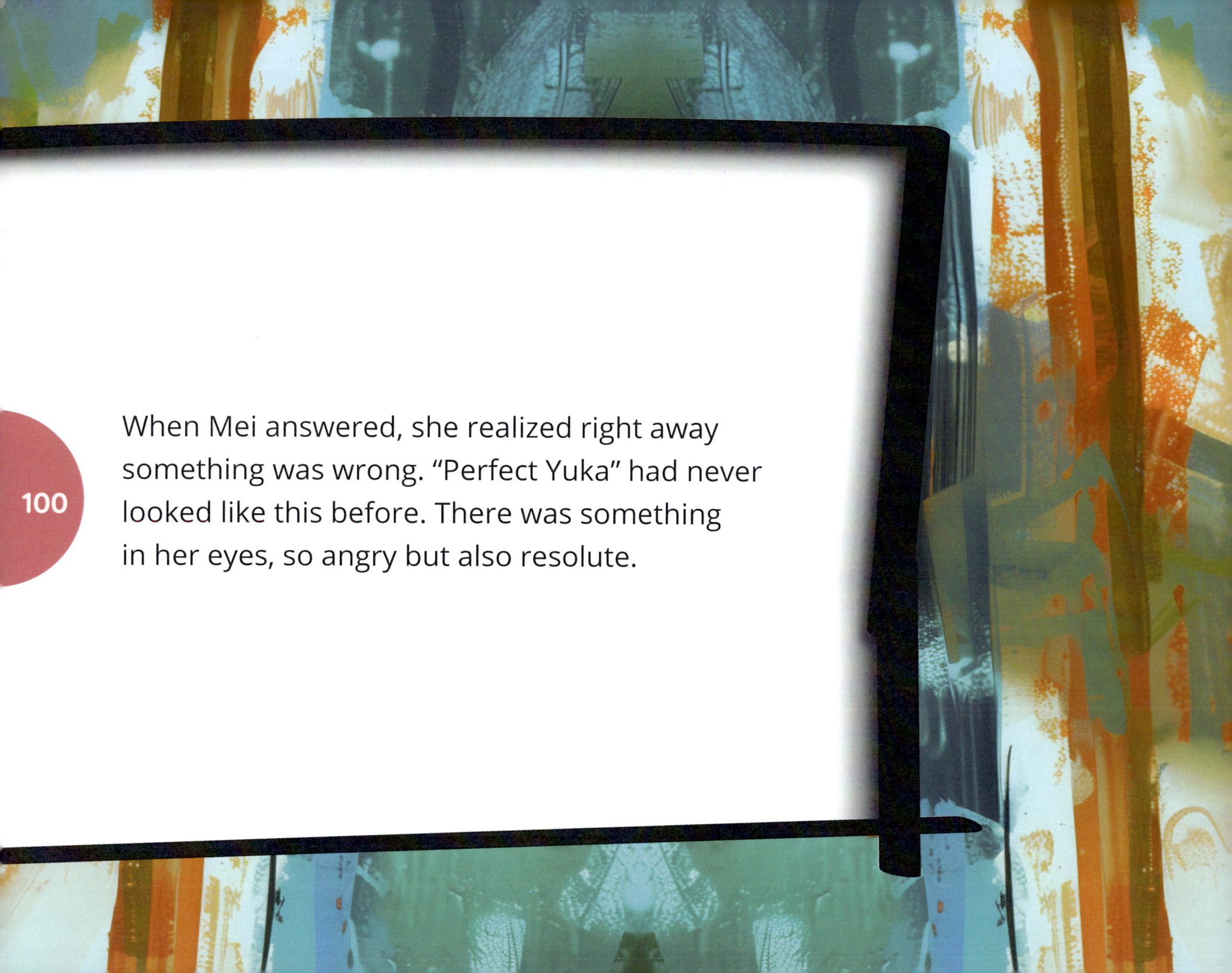

When Mei answered, she realized right away something was wrong. "Perfect Yuka" had never looked like this before. There was something in her eyes, so angry but also resolute.

101

102

In the weeks that followed, Yuka didn't say much to Mei, but she'd never seen this side of her sister before. There was a quiet power that felt so different than the frenetic energy she was used to. Mei's role was mainly to make sure Yuka was still remembering to eat as she navigated paperwork, meetings with lawyers, and the many phonecalls.

Yuka had decided this could never happen to anyone else again, at least in that workplace.

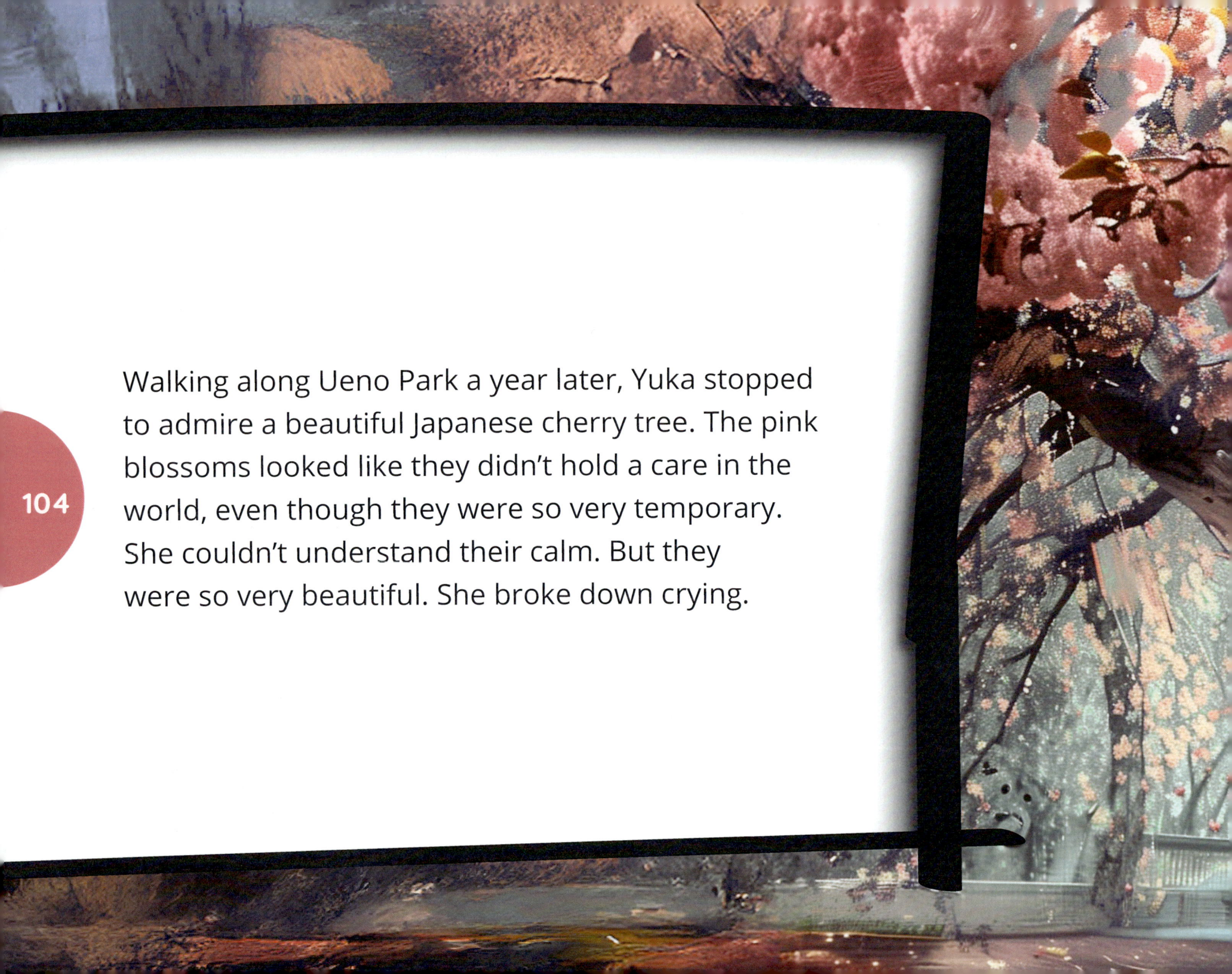

Walking along Ueno Park a year later, Yuka stopped to admire a beautiful Japanese cherry tree. The pink blossoms looked like they didn't hold a care in the world, even though they were so very temporary. She couldn't understand their calm. But they were so very beautiful. She broke down crying.

105

106

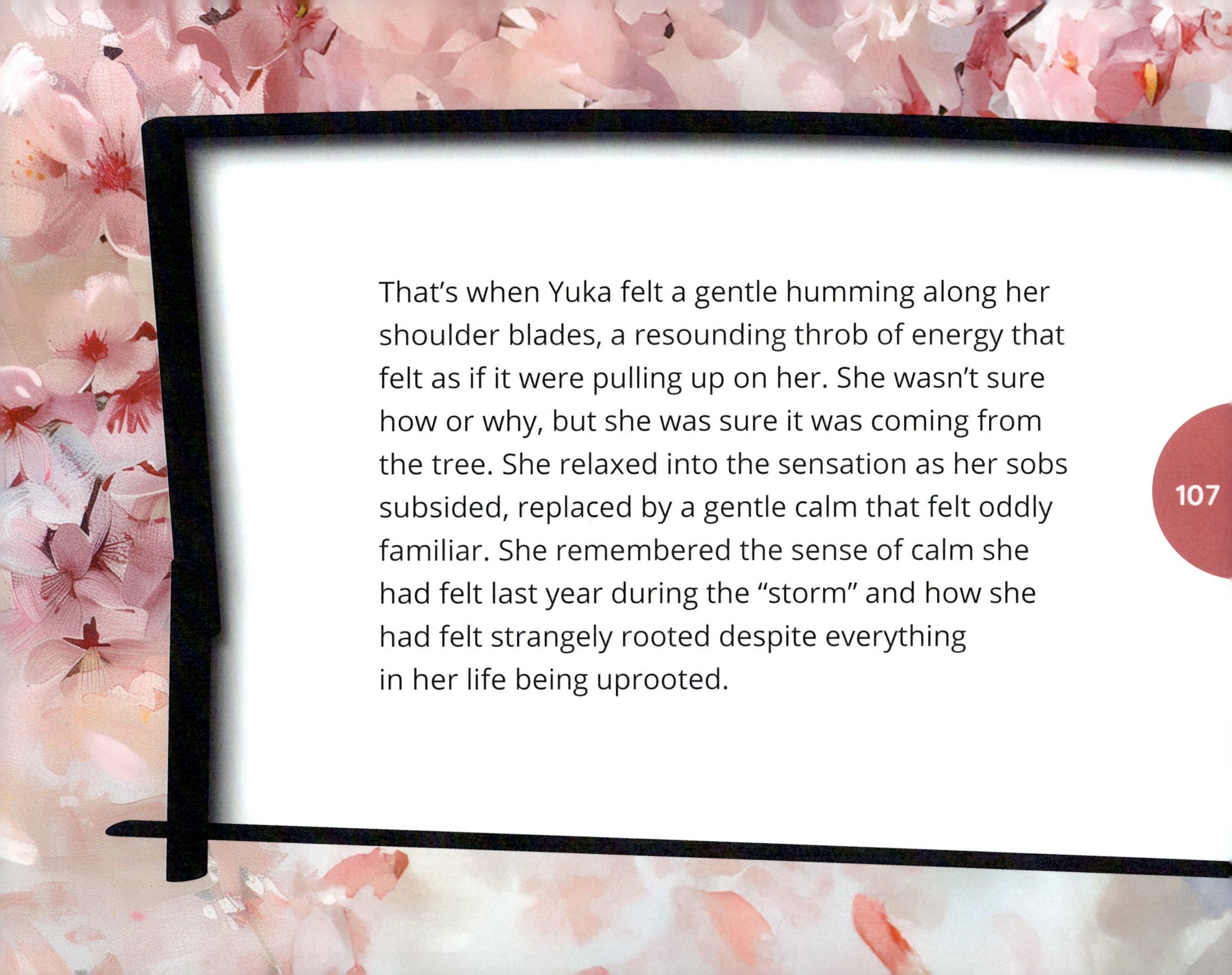

That's when Yuka felt a gentle humming along her shoulder blades, a resounding throb of energy that felt as if it were pulling up on her. She wasn't sure how or why, but she was sure it was coming from the tree. She relaxed into the sensation as her sobs subsided, replaced by a gentle calm that felt oddly familiar. She remembered the sense of calm she had felt last year during the "storm" and how she had felt strangely rooted despite everything in her life being uprooted.

Yuka smiled. It reminded her of an old poem she had read walking through a temple garden with her mama, so many years ago, before she became a young orphan.

Tree whispers gently,
Here is what is real, true.
Can you see it now?

She had not understood that poem until this very moment. As her soul swelled with joy, a bright light burst above her head, glowing beyond old memories, allowing them to fade into the background, and welcoming Yuka to her true Self.

109

111

She paused in front of a new door, feeling the energy vibrating off of it. She held out her hand and felt the surge of warmth coming from behind the door. She laughed to herself, deeply happy.

It was coming True.

Discussion Questions

You may wish to leverage these discussion questions as a tool to deepen your engagement with the text, either on your own or with others. Please use them however best serves you. For the character questions that resonate most deeply for you, we invite you to pause and reflect on your answer to them from both the character's story and from the perspective of your own personal life story.

Humphrey's Story

1. What was Humphrey running from when he was younger? How did this running evolve as he grew into adulthood? What happens as he stops running and fighting, and moves to acceptance?

2. What role do assumptions and beliefs play in Humphrey's life, both about himself and about others? How does letting go of old assumptions result in new kinds of learning for Humphrey?

3. What causes the arisings and disappearances of Felzer and Stanley in Humphrey's life? Consider this question beyond physical presence, i.e. including his awareness of them.

Bai Fei's Story

1. What stimulated Bai Fei during the early days of childhood? What shifted for Bai Fei as she came face-to-face with expectations and assumptions from the outside world?

2. What factors feed Bai Fei's feeling of being trapped? What experiences release her from it? What can this teach us about the nature of self-expression?

3. What does Suwon ultimately help Bai Fei sense within herself?

Yuka's Story

1. How does Yuka's energy shift from the beginning of the story to the end? What role does "Holly" play in this, and how does that evolve for Yuka? What can this teach us about the nature of personas?

2. What factors in Yuka's life support her transformation, both in painful ways and in loving ones? What can this teach us about the nature of transformation?

3. What truth does Yuka gain access to by the end of the story? How does this inform her understanding of her history? How can it continue to do so after the story ends?

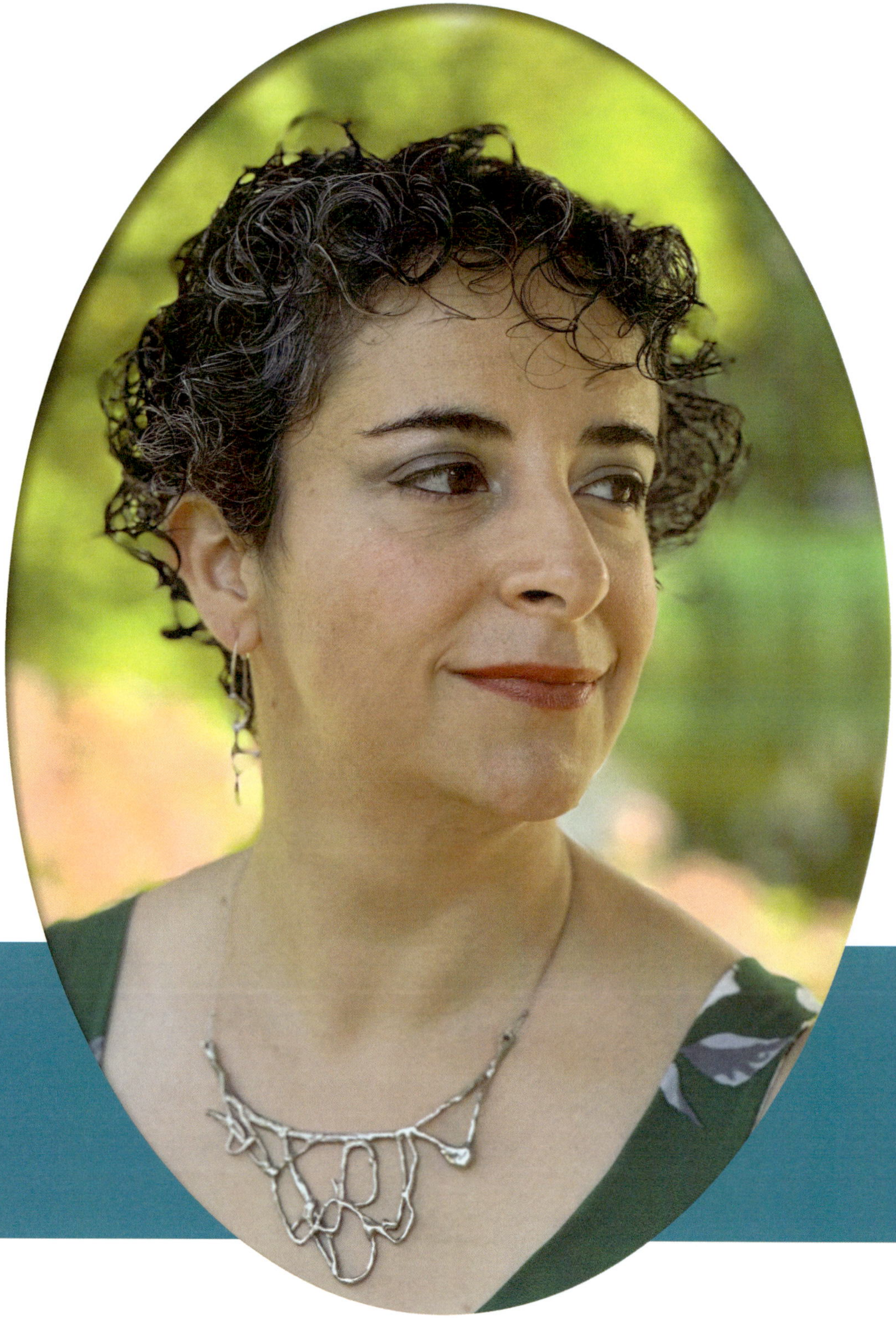

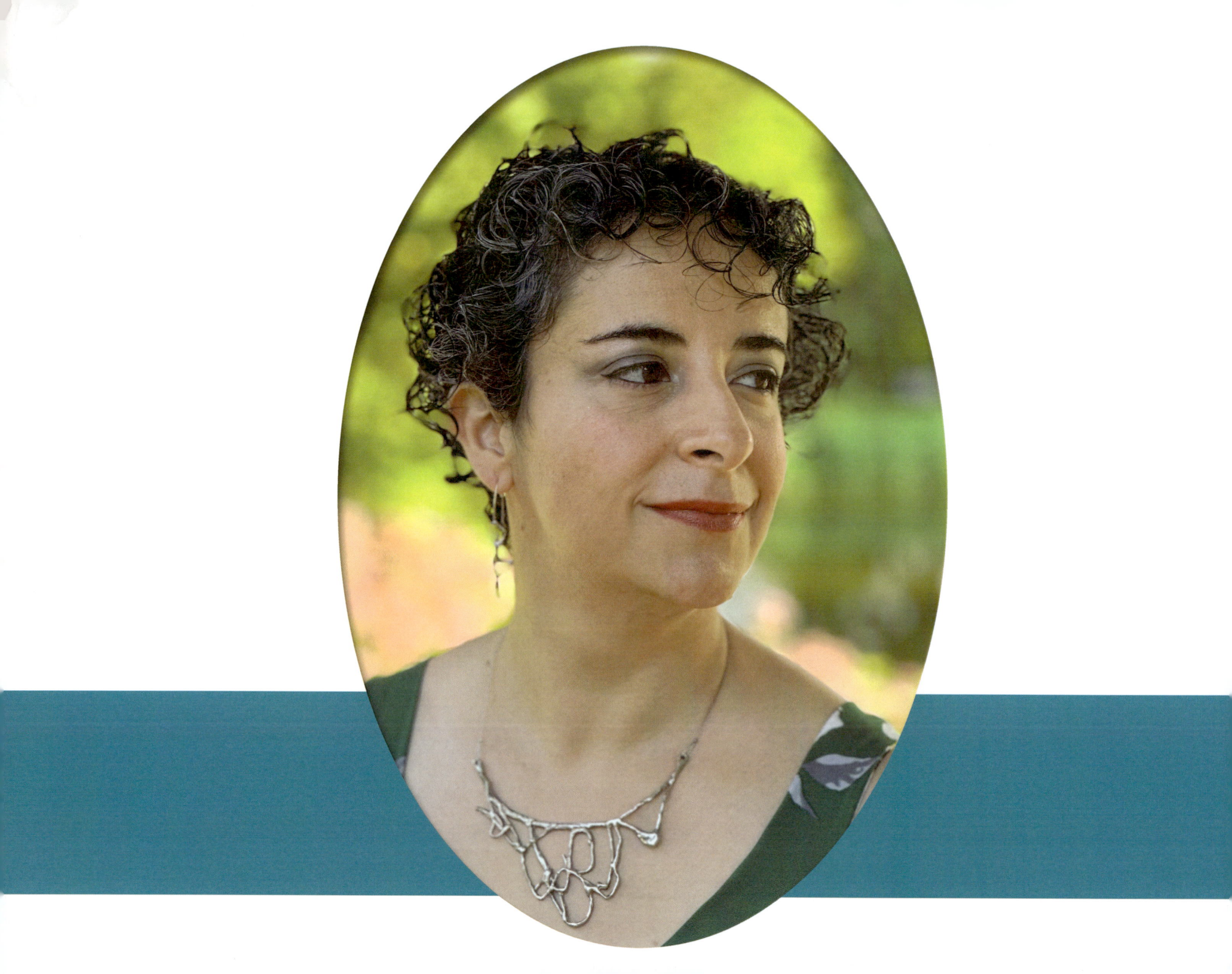

Dr. Loddie Foose (DocDocFoose) is a former political refugee and multinational business leader. A deep inner awakening resulted in her shifting her energy to philanthropic efforts and to helping others uncover their limitless potential. She travels the globe for impact and inspiration, capturing these stories on her journeys. Each story is informed by the unique energy of its respective locale.

   Loddie resides with her human and fur family in Colorado where she enjoys nature, exploration, and poetry.

She received her doctoral degree in chemical engineering from the University of California, Berkeley and completed her post-doctoral studies at Caltech (hence 'DocDocFoose').

Proceeds from this book support gender equity and food equity efforts. Together we're contributing toward something greater.

To learn more visit: **www.DocDocFoose.com**

Stay tuned for the next Soul Riders book, coming soon!

www.DocDocFoose.com